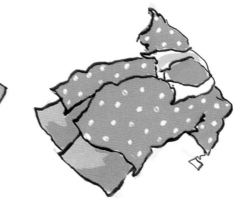
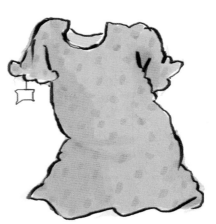

FIVE Little MONKEYS
go shopping

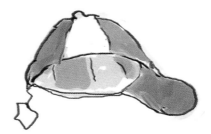

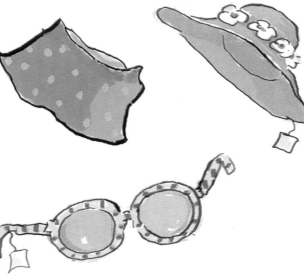

For Linda Cassidy
and her first grade monkeys

FIVE LITTLE MONKEYS ® is a registered trademark of Houghton Mifflin
Harcourt Publishing Company, and the monkey logo is a trademark of
Houghton Mifflin Harcourt Publishing Company.

All rights reserved. Published in the United States by Sandpiper, an imprint of
Houghton Mifflin Harcourt Publishing Company. Originally published in hardcover
in the United States by Clarion Books, an imprint of Houghton Mifflin Harcourt
Publishing Company, 2007.

SANDPIPER and the SANDPIPER logo are trademarks of
Houghton Mifflin Harcourt Publishing Company.

For information about permission to reproduce selections from this book, write to trade.
permissions@hmhco.com or to Permissions, Houghton Mifflin Harcourt Publishing
Company, 3 Park Avenue, 19th Floor, New York, New York 10016.

www.hmhco.com

The text of this book was set in 18-point Cantonia.
The illustrations were executed in digital pen and ink and acrylic gouache.

The Library of Congress has cataloged the hardcover edition as follows:
Christelow, Eileen.
Five little monkeys go shopping/by Eileen Christelow
p. cm.
Summary: Five little monkeys go shopping for school
clothes with their mama, but in spite of her warnings about
not wandering off, things quickly get complicated.
[1. Monkeys—Fiction. 2. Shopping—Fiction.] I. Title.
PZ7.C4523 Fig 2007
[E]—dc22 2006039523

ISBN: 978-0-618-82161-7 hardcover
ISBN: 978-0-547-74451-3 paperback

Manufactured in China
SCP 10 9 8 7

4500678907

FIVE Little MONKEYS
go shopping

EILEEN CHRISTELOW

sandpiper

Houghton Mifflin Harcourt
Boston   New York

The day before school starts, Mama takes her five little monkeys shopping for clothes. "Stick with me," she says, "and don't go wandering off!"

BACK TO SC

"We need dresses, pants, shirts, hats, and backpacks for my five little monkeys," says Mama.

"But I see only four little monkeys," says the saleslady.

"1 2 3 4."

"You four little monkeys try on these clothes while I go find her. But stay right here, and DON'T GO WANDERING OFF!"

11

So one little monkey tries on pants.
Two little monkeys try on shirts.
One little monkey tries on a dress.

Then two of those monkeys are so thirsty! They want to find a water fountain.

Off they go . . . just as Mama comes
back with the one missing monkey.

"Now I have my five little monkeys!" Mama says.
"But I see only three little monkeys," says the saleslady.

"1 2 3."

"Only three little monkeys?" gasps Mama.
"Am I missing more monkeys?
How can that be?"

5 little monkeys
- 3 monkeys here
_____
= 2 missing monkeys

"I need to find those two little monkeys!"
says Mama. "You three little monkeys
can try on more clothes, but
STAY RIGHT HERE, AND
DON'T GO WANDERING OFF!"

So those three little monkeys are looking for more clothes when they see three monkey friends.

Then one of the little monkeys needs to find a bathroom.

Off he goes . . . just as Mama hurries back with her two missing monkeys. "Now I have my five little monkeys," she says.

"But I see seven little monkeys," says the saleslady.

"1 2 3 4 5 6 7."

"Seven little monkeys?" gasps Mama. "How can that be?"

"We found three friends!" two of her little monkeys explain. "Their papa has gone to look for their two little sisters!"

"Oh, no!" says Mama.
"I'm so confused! Am I STILL missing a monkey?"

"I need to find my one little monkey," says Mama. "You seven little monkeys try on more clothes. STAY RIGHT HERE, AND DON'T GO WANDERING OFF!"

But the four little monkeys and their three monkey friends get tired of trying on clothes. "Let's go help Mama!" they say.

Off they go . . . just as Mama hurries back with her one missing monkey, the monkey friends' papa, and their two little sister monkeys.

"Now we have ten little monkeys," says Mama.
"But I see only three little monkeys," says the saleslady.

"1 2 3."

"Oh, no!" wails Mama. "Am I still missing some monkeys? How can that be?"

"STAY RIGHT HERE!" says the saleslady. "AND DON'T GO WANDERING OFF!"

Then the saleslady makes an announcement. "Will all the little monkeys who are missing their mamas, papas, little sisters or brothers please come to the children's clothing department RIGHT NOW!"

Lots of little monkeys hurry to the children's clothing department.

"Now I have my five little monkeys," says Mama.
"And I have my five little monkeys," says the monkey
friends' papa. "So we have ten little monkeys!"

"No," says the saleslady.

"You have fourteen little monkeys.

1 2 3 4 5 6 7 8 9 10 11 12 13 14.

You have four extra little monkeys."

"Those four belong to me!"
cries a grandma monkey.

33

"Now that everyone has found everybody, would anyone like to buy anything?" asks the saleslady.

The five little monkeys and Mama buy dresses,
pants, hats, shorts, backpacks, and sunglasses,
and then they head for the car.

Can I play at your house?

Sure!

"At last, we've finished our shopping," says Mama.
"And at last, I have all of my five little monkeys!"

"No, you have six," says one little monkey.

"1 2 3 4 5 6."

How can THAT be?

SCREECH!

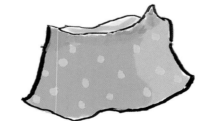